Little Critter's Bedtime Storybook

By Mercer Mayer

A GOLDEN BOOK • NEW YORK

Western Publishing Company, Inc., Racine, Wisconsin 53404

CONTENTS

BEDTIME

"It's getting late," said Mom.

"It's time for bed," said Dad.

"I should get to go to bed later," said Little Critter, "because I'm older."

"I don't want to go upstairs alone!" Little Sister complained.

"She keeps me awake," said Little Critter.

"I do not, I go right to sleep," said Little Sister.

But Dad settled the argument. "You're both going to bed, so go on."

Little Critter and Little Sister marched upstairs, put on their pajamas, brushed their teeth, and got into bed.

"Good night, sleep tight," said Mom and Dad.

THE FUSSY PRINCESS

"I can't sleep without my bear," Little Sister complained.

"Where is it?"

"I think I left it downstairs."

Little Critter yawned. "So go and get it."

"I'm scared to go downstairs alone," Little Sister whined.

Little Critter sighed and went to get Little Sister's bear. He handed it to her and got back into bed.

"This isn't the right bear." Little Sister frowned. "I want the pink one."

"What's the difference?" asked Little Critter.

"This is the brown one. I play outside with this one. I sleep with the *pink* one."

"Okay, okay." Little Critter groaned. "If I get the pink one, will you go to sleep?"

"Yes." Little Sister nodded.

This time Little Critter brought her the pink bear. He got into bed one more time.

"I think my fuzzy blanket is downstairs, too," said Little Sister.

"Why didn't you tell me that before?" grumbled Little Critter.

"I didn't think of it," said Little Sister.

"You don't need it," said Little Critter.

"I do, too," insisted Little Sister.

"You do not," Little Critter said sharply. "You don't need all that stuff in your bed to sleep."

"Yes, I do. I need my bear *and* my fuzzy blanket or I can't sleep at all."

"You are too fussy," Little Critter said.

"Did you say I was fuzzy?"

"No, fussy, fussy, fussy," said Little Critter.

"What does 'fussy' mean?" asked Little Sister.

"I'll tell you a story about a fussy princess, and then you'll know," answered Little Critter.

"What does this have to do with my fuzzy blanket?" asked Little Sister.

"Do you want to hear the story or not?" Little Critter demanded.

"Oh, okay," said Little Sister.

Little Critter began to tell the story.

"Once upon a time, a long, long time ago, there was a fussy princess who couldn't sleep unless everything was just right. She had to have all her favorite dolls propped on the bed in just the right order. She had to have her favorite blanket, and the sheets had to be perfectly smooth."

"You're telling a story about me. I don't like stories that are about me," said Little Sister.

"Are you a princess who lived a long, long time ago?" asked Little Critter.

"Well, no," admitted Little Sister.

"Then this story is not about you," Little Critter explained. "So, do you want to hear it or not?"

"All right, go on," said Little Sister.

"Here we go, then," said Little Critter. "This princess had to have everything just so at night. If the window was open too much, she had to have it shut. If the air was too still, someone had to fan her. And everyone in the castle had to be quiet and tippy-toe around after she went to bed, because the least little noise would disturb her.

"She was no picnic during the day, either. All of her dresses had to be perfectly pressed. If they had even the slightest wrinkle, she hollered and threw a fit. She had royal maids ironing her clothes all day.

"Oh, and if she fell down," Little Critter added, "she screamed and screamed."

Little Sister shook her head. "I scream when I fall down but never if my dress is wrinkled."

Little Critter kept telling the story. "One day a big dragon who lived in the mountains flew down to the castle. He had heard about the fussy princess and how the servants took care of her. It sounded like a good deal to him, and he liked the castle when he saw it. So he decided to move in.

"The first thing he did was throw out the king and his family."
"Are dragons real?" asked Little Sister.
"Not anymore," said Little Critter.
"Were dragons fussy?" she asked.

"Just listen, will you?" said Little Critter. "The royal family spent the first night in a barn. The princess had to sleep with cows, donkeys, sheep, and chickens. Needless to say, she didn't sleep a wink and in the morning she was in a very bad mood."

"I wouldn't want to sleep with a cow," Little Sister said with a shudder.

"I'm sure a cow wouldn't want to sleep with you, either," said Little Critter.

"Anyhow," Little Critter said, "when the farmer found them the next morning, he threw them out for trespassing. That night they had to sleep under a tree."

"I bet it rained," Little Sister chimed in.

"That's right." Little Critter nodded. "It rained and they got all wet. The princess didn't sleep well that night, either.

"By the third night the princess was a cranky mess. Her fur was all matted with mud. Her nice gown was all torn and dirty. And was it ever wrinkled! This was just too much. Not only had her family been thrown out of the castle and forced to live under a tree, not only was her only dress ruined, but the dragon had her favorite blanket and all of her dolls. So she hollered and threw a fit. She yelled and screamed until her father promised to go and get her things from the dragon."

"When I holler and scream, Daddy makes *me* go sit in our room," said Little Sister.

"Well, the princess didn't have a room anymore, so I guess her daddy felt bad for her," said Little Critter.

"Her father went back to the castle, pounded on the door, and told the dragon to open up. And that's just what the dragon did—he opened the door. Then he blew his fiery breath at the king and chased him away. The king went back to his family under the tree, defeated and slightly scorched. So the princess made up her mind to be brave and do something herself."

"What did she do?" Little Sister asked.

"She decided to sneak into the castle that night when everyone was asleep and get her favorite dolls and blanket," answered Little Critter.

"It was very late when she reached the castle," he continued. "She snuck upstairs to her room. To her surprise she found the dragon sleeping in her bed, with her favorite blanket, and all her dolls propped around him. Boy, did she get mad."

"Wasn't she scared?" Little Sister wondered.

"Of course she was," Little Critter told her, "but she was even more angry than she was scared.

"But, you know, that dragon had smoke pouring out of his nose and he did look awfully ferocious," Little Critter added.

"Does 'ferocious' mean fussy?" Little Sister wanted to know.

"No, no, no. 'Ferocious' means fierce," explained Little Critter, and he went on with his story. "The princess was so mad, she went to the laundry room and got a big bucket full of soapy water. Then she went upstairs and threw it right in the sleeping dragon's face. The dragon woke up with a snort and a sputter.

"'Now you're gonna get it,' the dragon said to the princess.

"He got out of bed and drew himself up tall. He glared at the princess with his big yellow eyes and showed her his fangs. *Now* the princess was more scared than angry," said Little Critter. "She started to back away toward the door. The dragon puffed himself up and began to blow fire at her—but all that came out were soapy bubbles! The princess had put out his fire."

"Did the dragon cry?" asked Little Sister.

"Yes, he did," said Little Critter. "No one had ever put out his fire before, and without it he couldn't be ferocious. So he cried and cried.

"The king and the queen were worried sick when they discovered that the princess was missing. They thought she had probably gone to the castle, so they ran there as fast as they could. You can imagine how surprised they were when they burst into the room and found their daughter comforting a crying dragon."

"Were they mean to the dragon?" asked Little Sister.

"No, they weren't," Little Critter reassured her. "After he apologized for being so awful, they invited him to stay on as a guest.

"Well," Little Critter went on and finished up the story, "the princess was so happy to have her favorite blanket and all her dolls back again, and she was so happy to be back in the castle, that she decided not to be fussy anymore. After living under a tree, she realized it didn't matter if her favorite blanket wasn't in just the right spot, or if one of her dolls was in another room, or if someone made a little noise when she was trying to sleep."

"Is that all?" asked Little Sister.

"That's it," said Little Critter. "Now go to sleep."

"But I can't sleep without my fuzzy blanket," said Little Sister.

"Didn't you understand the story?" Little Critter asked.

"Yes, I did," replied Little Sister, "but *I'm* not a princess and there is no dragon in *my* bed."

"If I get your fuzzy blanket," Little Critter asked, "do you promise to go to sleep?"

"Yes, if you also get me a drink of water on the way back."

THE BEAR WHO
WOULDN'T SHARE

"What are you doing?" Little Critter asked.
"Nothing," said Little Sister. *Munch, munch.*
"You're eating something," said Little Critter.
"No, I'm not," said Little Sister. *Munch, munch.*
"Give me a cookie," said Little Critter.
"No!"
"Did you ever hear the story of the bear who wouldn't share?"
asked Little Critter.
"No!"
"Then I'm going to tell it to you," said Little Critter.

MUNCH!
MUNCH!

"Once upon a time Mr. Bear gathered up all the food he would need to last him through the long cold winter and stored it in the back of his snug cave. The bear had barrels full of apples and berries, so he made all the pies and jams and good things he could possibly want when he woke up in the spring. You see, bears eat a lot in the fall so they can sleep all winter. And the bear wanted to be sure there'd be a big breakfast waiting for him.

"He ate a great big dinner, put on his soft pajamas with fuzzy feet, and crawled into bed all ready to snuggle down for a long winter's sleep. But he hadn't dozed off for more than a month when he was awakened by a loud knocking at his door. He struggled to his feet and stumbled to the front door. He unbolted it and opened it wide. There, huddled on his doorstep, was a half-frozen little critter."

"Who did the little critter look like?" Little Sister interrupted.

"What do you mean?" asked Little Critter.

"Was it you or me?" Little Sister said.

"Uh, me," said Little Critter.

"Good. I don't like the cold," said Little Sister.

"Well, the little critter spoke to the bear. He said, 'Please, Mr. Bear, would you let me come in? It has been the coldest winter ever, and I'm half frozen and half starved.'

"This wasn't at all what the bear had in mind when he settled down for a long winter's sleep, but he said, 'You can come in if you'd like, but I'm just a poor bear and I have very little to eat.'"

"That's not true!" Little Sister cried. "He had all those apples and all that other stuff he was saving!"

"I know," said Little Critter. "Just be quiet and listen. The bear let the little critter sleep on a small rug by the fireplace. Then he crawled back into his own bed and fell into a deep, deep sleep. Suddenly he was awakened by another banging on the door. Now there was a family of cold and hungry rabbits on his doorstep. The rabbits asked if they could come in and have something to eat.

"The bear told them, 'I will let you in to warm yourselves, but I can't spare anything to eat.' So the rabbits snuggled down into a big washtub lined with a blanket. Then the bear went back to sleep."

"I don't like that bear," said Little Sister, reaching for another cookie.

25

"He was pretty selfish," agreed Little Critter. "Before long there was still more banging on the door. This time there were beavers, deer, skunks, otters, and all sorts of forest animals on the doorstep. Before they could say a word, the bear said, 'You can come in if you want to, but there's no food.'

"The cave was very crowded by this time, but everyone found a place to sleep. Then the bear crawled back into his bed. As he dropped off to sleep he could hear the little animals crying because they were so hungry."

"Do bears dream?" Little Sister wondered.

"Sure," said Little Critter. "As a matter of fact, this bear had a dream that very night."

"What did he dream?" asked Little Sister.

"He dreamed that his conscience came to visit him," said Little Critter.

"What's a conscience?" asked Little Sister.

"That's the part of you that tells you to be fair and to do good things," explained Little Critter.

"Oh," said Little Sister.

Little Critter went on. "The conscience told the bear that he was very selfish and stingy and asked how he could just lie there in bed like a big lump of fur and let all the other animals starve. The bear tried to stick up for himself. He said, 'If I feed them all, I won't have anything left to eat in the spring when I wake up. Then *I'll* be hungry.'

"'Sweet dreams to you, then,' grumbled the conscience—and disappeared.

"But his dreams weren't sweet," said Little Critter. "They were about all those hungry animals. Suddenly he woke up and looked around. Then, with a shout, he jumped out of bed. 'I just remembered,' he said, 'I have a whole storeroom full of apples, berries, pies, jams, and everything good to eat.' He threw open the storeroom door and told everyone to dig in. When all the animals had eaten, the bear invited everyone to either stay or take what they needed to eat. Then he went back to bed and slept soundly.

"Finally spring came and the bear woke up. He yawned, rubbed his eyes, and looked around the room. No one was there. They had all gone back to their own homes. He looked in the storeroom, but all that was left was one little wrinkled apple. The bear was terribly hungry, and he was wondering what he was going to do when he noticed a pile of letters that had been stuck under his door. He opened one and read it.

"It said:

> Dear Mr. Bear:
>   I want to thank you for being so generous this past winter
> and for sharing your wonderful food. When you wake up in the
> spring, you must come to my house for breakfast.
>   Sincerely,
>   the little critter
>   who stayed in your cave

"The bear opened another letter," said Little Critter, "and it was a dinner invitation. In another one someone promised to bring a feast right to his cave. Each and every letter was more wonderful than the last. A big tear came to Mr. Bear's eye, and he thought, 'Why, I have everything I could ever want this spring—food *and* friends.'"

"Here," said Little Sister, passing him the box of cookies.
"Hey! There's only one cookie left!" said Little Critter.
"That's because you told such a long story," Little Sister answered.

THE DAY THE WIND STOPPED BLOWING

"Quit turning the light on," said Little Critter.

"But I'm scared," said Little Sister.

"Of what?"

"The wind," said Little Sister. "It's blowing so hard that it's scaring me. I *need* the light on when I'm scared."

"But I can't sleep with it on," said Little Critter. He thought for a moment. Then he said, "Did you ever hear the story of the day the wind stopped blowing?"

"No," said Little Sister. "Will you tell it to me?"

"Sure," said Little Critter, and he began.

30

"Once upon a time the wind blew even harder than he does now."

"Why did he blow so hard?" asked Little Sister.

"It made him feel good," said Little Critter. "He could blow so hard that birds had trouble flying and people had trouble walking. Sometimes he even blew the roofs right off the houses. And people couldn't have picnics, because all the food would get blown away.

"As time went by, people got tired of the wind blowing so hard. They began to complain to the king."

"Why? The king didn't do anything," said Little Sister.

"No, but he was the king, and the king was supposed to fix everything," answered Little Critter.

"Oh," said Little Sister.

"The king tried his best to stop the wind," said Little Critter. "He had a high wall built around the kingdom, but the wind blew so hard that the wall fell down. Next the king sent the royal army out to stop the wind, but the wind blew them back. Then the king got mad and threw a temper tantrum—but that didn't do any good, either."

"I do that sometimes," said Little Sister.

"Does it do any good?" asked Little Critter.

"Sometimes," said Little Sister.

Little Critter went on. "Well, then the king had signs tacked up on all the trees, offering a huge reward to anyone who could get the wind to stop blowing. But the wind blew the signs down before anyone could see them."

"It sounds like he was mean," said Little Sister.

"No, he wasn't," said Little Critter. "I told you, blowing hard made him feel good. He didn't know he was causing trouble.

"Anyway, it just so happened that one of the signs blew right into the house of a little mouse and landed in his soup. After he had gotten over his surprise, the mouse pulled out the sign and read it. He thought, 'I'll go to the palace and tell the king that *I* will get the wind to stop blowing.'"

"Did the mouse know how to do that?" asked Little Sister.

"He wasn't sure," said Little Critter, "but he was tired of having things blow into his soup, and he hoped to win the reward money. He was a poor mouse."

"Oh," said Little Sister.

"When the mouse arrived at the palace and told the king his plans, the king just laughed at him. He didn't believe a little mouse could succeed where the king had failed. So he threw the mouse out of the castle. Well, now the little mouse was really mad. He was more determined than ever to find the wind and get him to stop blowing. He set out that very day. He walked for miles. The wind was blowing harder and harder, and it wasn't easy for the mouse to stay on his feet, so he knew he was going the right way. Finally he got to the wind's house and knocked on the door."

"How did he know?" asked Little Sister.

"Know what?" said Little Critter.

"That the wind lived there," said Little Sister.

"It was a good guess," said Little Critter. "Anyway, the wind didn't get a lot of visitors, so he invited the little mouse in."

"How come the wind didn't have visitors?" Little Sister wanted to know.

"Because people like you thought he was mean. Now be quiet and listen. The little mouse was tired and mad, so he didn't waste any time. He yelled at the wind and told him what a nuisance he was. He told him not to blow anymore, because no one appreciated being knocked around. He said he was acting like a bully and a meany."

"What did the wind do?"

"Well, the wind was very surprised to hear all this, and his feelings were hurt. Without saying a word, he went upstairs and closed the door.

"After the wind left, the little mouse noticed that the air had become very still. Not even a tiny breeze was blowing. 'Hooray! I did it—I got the wind to stop!' he thought.

"Very pleased with himself, the little mouse started back to the castle to collect his reward. But along the way he noticed how hot it was now that there was no wind. And because there was nothing to blow the clouds away, it started to rain. No boats were moving on the ocean, because there was no wind to push their sails. No kites were flying. Nobody looked happy.

"When the sweaty little mouse marched into the throne room and demanded his reward," Little Critter continued, "the king glared at him. He wasn't convinced that the mouse had been the one who made the wind stop, and besides, he thought things were even worse than before. He threatened to put the mouse in the dungeon. This time the mouse didn't wait to get tossed out. He ran out of the castle as fast as he could, all the way back to the wind's house. He knocked and

knocked, but the wind wouldn't come to the door. Finally the wind peeked out of an upstairs window and said, 'Go away. Nobody likes me.'

"The mouse asked the wind to come down so they could talk things over. He apologized for being so rude before and told the wind how important he was to everyone. The wind cheered up a little. He agreed to start blowing again so long as every once in a while he was allowed to blow as hard as he liked. The mouse stayed for a while and helped the wind to practice blowing until he knew what was just right and what was too hard.

"The little mouse went back to the king and demanded his reward again," said Little Critter. "The king just laughed and laughed. But suddenly the sky grew dark and a great big storm blew right into the castle. 'ARE YOU LAUGHING AT MY LITTLE FRIEND?' bellowed the wind. He had followed the mouse to the castle.

"The king turned white as a sheet. 'Errr, why, no,' he muttered. 'I was laughing because I am so happy to give him a big reward.'

"'BE SURE THAT YOU DO,' boomed the wind, who winked at his friend and then blew himself home.

"The king, true to his word, gave the little mouse a big reward and made him the official royal weathermouse. And everyone was happy most of the time except when the wind decided not to blow at all, or when he blew as hard as he could. So you see, everyone learned that the wind is friendly, and not scary at all."

"Is that the end of the story?" asked Little Sister.

"Yes, now go to sleep," said Little Critter.

"Do you think the wind likes me?" Little Sister asked.

"He likes you at least as much as I do," answered Little Critter.

"Okay, then," said Little Sister. She turned off the light and settled down. "Good night, wind," she whispered.

THE GRUMPY OLD RABBIT

"I can't sleep," grumbled Little Sister. "My bed is too lumpy and my pillow is too hard."

"Did you ever hear the story of the grumpy old rabbit?" asked Little Critter.

"No, and I don't want to hear it."

"Too bad," said Little Critter. "It's a really good story."

"Okay, tell me a little bit of it," said Little Sister.

"Once upon a time there was a grumpy old rabbit who lived in a little rabbit hole under a great big oak tree. And he didn't like anything. He didn't like his snug little rabbit hole because he thought it was too small and musty…"

"Musty?" interrupted Little Sister.

"That means his house smelled funny," explained Little Critter.

"Oh!" said Little Sister.

Little Critter went on. "Well, this old rabbit didn't like his armchair, either. He thought it was too hard. And he thought his living room rug was too tattered and worn. He didn't like his kitchen because the stove was so old and the sink was cracked. And when he went to sleep, he complained about his bed because he didn't think it was fluffy enough."

"You know," Little Sister said, "my bed's not fluffy, either."

"I know," said Little Critter. "That's why I'm telling you this story. Guess what happened next?"

"Tell me," said Little Sister.

"He was just so miserable," said Little Critter, "that he decided to go and live with his niece and her family. But his niece had a rabbit hole even smaller than his own, and she and her husband had seven noisy little rabbits. At dinnertime there were so many mouths to feed that the old rabbit barely got anything to eat. And when bedtime came, he discovered that he had to share a bed with three squiggly little rabbits. Needless to say, they kicked, bounced, and squirmed all night long. The grumpy old rabbit didn't sleep a wink."

"Why didn't they just buy him a bed?" asked Little Sister.

"They were very poor," answered Little Critter.

"Oh!" said Little Sister.

"After three nights of this," Little Critter said, "the grumpy old rabbit had had enough. He decided to go and live with his rich nephew and his wife, who had only one baby bunny. When he arrived, you can imagine how happy he was to find a spacious rabbit hole with all the modern conveniences—hot and cold running water, three bathrooms, and best of all, a large bedroom for him alone, with the biggest, fluffiest bed he had ever felt in his whole life."

"I bet he was really happy now," said Little Sister.

"He was for a while," Little Critter told her. "But his nephew's wife was very mean. She made the old rabbit get out of bed first thing in the morning so the maid could make the bed and straighten the room. This nephew's wife nagged at him whenever he picked anything up because she was afraid that he might break it. She made him wear a tie and jacket to dinner. And he had to be very, very quiet all the time so that he wouldn't disturb the baby. After two days of this silliness, the old rabbit decided to go and live with his elderly sister, who lived all alone."

"That sounds better to me," Little Sister commented.

"Just wait and see," Little Critter warned her. "Well, his elderly sister was just so pleased to have him come, because now she would have someone to do things for her. That night he slept on the hardest bed ever. And when morning came, he had to make both beds. Then he had to make breakfast, wash the dishes, and do all the chores—take out the garbage, cut wood, and paint the barn. By the end of the first day the grumpy old rabbit looked around at all the work that he had left to do. He thought that if he were back in his own little home, with his own lumpy little bed, he would never be grumpy again. So he decided to go home."

"What did he do when he got there?"

"Well," said Little Critter, "he opened the front door and went into his shabby, musty little rabbit hole. But it looked better than anything he had ever seen. He was so tired that he went straight to his bedroom. He put on his nightshirt and turned down the covers. As he crawled into his lumpy bed he thought, 'At least it's mine. And this musty old rabbit hole is mine. And I can do just as I please here.' That thought made him so happy that a big smile spread across his face as he drifted off into the best sleep he ever had.

"Now you go to sleep, too!" finished Little Critter.

"What's the matter now?" asked Little Critter when he saw the grumpy look on Little Sister's face.

"My bed is *still* too lumpy, but your story has made me so sleepy, I think I'll go to sleep anyway." Little Sister yawned and snuggled under the covers.

"Good. And good night," answered Little Critter.